TWISTERS

KU-673-459

UNDERSEA ADVENTURE

Paul Harrison
and Barbara Nascimbeni

Evans

Swim with me under the sea.

6

Whose eye is that?

Whale!

Down through the weeds.

11

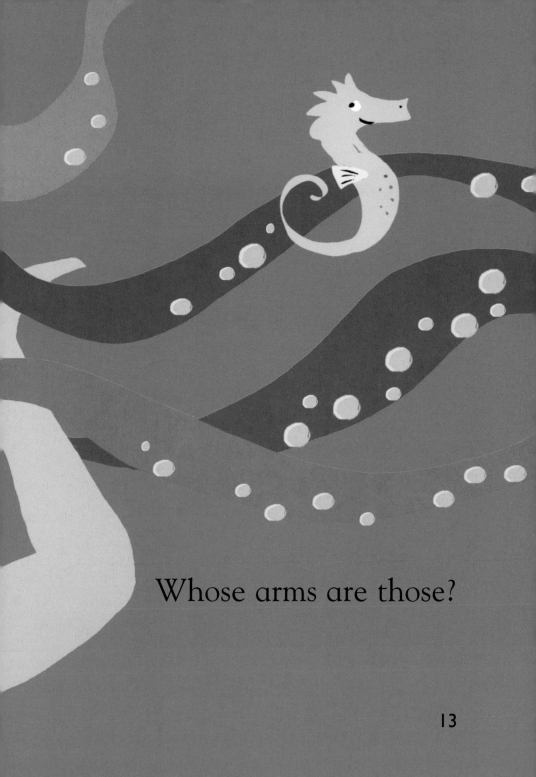

Whose arms are those?

Octopus!

15

16

Down to the sea bed.

18

What's in the box?

20

Treasure!

Whose teeth are those?

22

23

Shark!

24

Quick! Up to the surface.

26

Into the boat!

29

Out of reach, safe on
the beach.

Why not try reading another Twisters book?

Not-so-silly Sausage by Stella Gurney and Liz Million 978 0237 52875 1

Nick's Birthday by Jane Oliver and Silvia Raga 978 0237 52896 6

Out Went Sam by Nick Turpin and Barbara Nascimbeni 978 0237 52894 2

Yummy Scrummy by Paul Harrison and Belinda Worsley 978 0237 52876 8

Squelch! by Kay Woodward and Stefania Colnaghi 978 0237 52895 9

Sally Sails the Seas by Stella Gurney and Belinda Worsely 978 0237 52893 5

Billy on the Ball by Paul Harrison and Silvia Raga 978 0237 52926 0

Countdown by Kay Woodward and Ofra Amit 978 0237 52927 7

One Wet Welly by Gill Matthews and Belinda Worsley 978 0237 52928 4

Sand Dragon by Su Swallow and Silvia Raga 978 0237 52929 1

Cave-baby and the Mammoth by Vivian French and Lisa Williams 978 0237 52931 4

Albert Liked Ladders by Su Swallow and Tim Archbold 978 0237 52930 7

Molly is New by Nick Turpin and Silvia Raga 978 0237 53067 9

A Head Full of Stories by Su Swallow and Tim Archbold 978 0237 53069 3

Elephant Rides Again by Paul Harrison and Liz Million 978 0237 53073 0

Bird Watch by Su Swallow and Simona Dimitri 978 0237 53071 6

Pip Likes Snow by Lynne Rickards and Belinda Worsely 978 0237 53075 4

How to Build a House by Nick Turpin and Barbara Nascimbeni 978 0237 53065 5

Hattie the Dancing Hippo by Jillian Powell and Emma Dodson 978 0237 53335 9

Mary Had a Dinosaur by Eileen Browne and Ruth Rivers 978 0237 53337 3

When I Was a Baby by Madeline Goodey and Amy Brown 978 0237 53334 2

Will's Boomerang by Stella Gurney and Stefania Colnaghi 978 0237 53336 6

Birthday Boy by Dereen Taylor and Ruth Rivers 978 0237 53469 1

Mr Bickle and the Ghost by Stella Gurney and Silvia Raga 978 0237 53465 3

Noisy Books by Paul Harrison and Fabiano Fiorin 978 0237 53467 7

Undersea Adventure by Paul Harrison and Barbara Nascimbeni 978 0237 53463 9